35 STORIES IN 1

GIANT
TREASURY
FOR 4 YEAR OLDS

Written by Deborah Chancellor,
Lizzie Irvin, Jillian Harker, Jan Payne and Nick Ellsworth

Illustrated by Andy Catling, Eva Musynski
and Diana Catchpole

This edition published by Parragon in 2010

Parragon
Queen Street House
4 Queen Street
Bath BA1 1HE, UK

ISBN 978-1-4454-1111-8

Printed in Canada.

35 STORIES IN 1

GIANT
TREASURY
FOR 4 YEAR OLDS

PaRragon

Bath · New York · Singapore · Hong Kong · Cologne · Delhi · Melbourne

Contents

The New Rocket

Zack stared out of the window at Mom's brand-new space rocket parked on the Moon's surface. It had blue and silver stripes and shone in the starlight.

Zack *really* wanted to fly it. But he knew Mom wouldn't let him.

Mom put on her space helmet. "I'm off to the space station now, Zack," she said. "Be good." She stepped into the teleporter, and disappeared into thin air.

Zack looked at the space rocket. "I could fly that rocket now," he said to himself. "I bet it's really easy." He put on his space suit, went out to the rocket and slid open the door. Mom had left the starter crystal in the ignition pad.

Once the door was safely closed, Zack
took off his helmet and pushed down the
crystal. The rocket's engines fired up.
Zack gulped. It was now or never. "I'll be
back by lunch time," he thought. He took
a deep breath and took off.

At first everything seemed easy. Zack
made it safely past planet Earth, and
began to head for Mars.

But then a comet came rushing towards
Zack. He hit the SOS button and grabbed
the controls, but he couldn't make the
rocket swerve away quickly enough.

He was going to crash!

"What on earth are you doing, you naughty boy?"

It was Mom! She was right next to Zack.

12

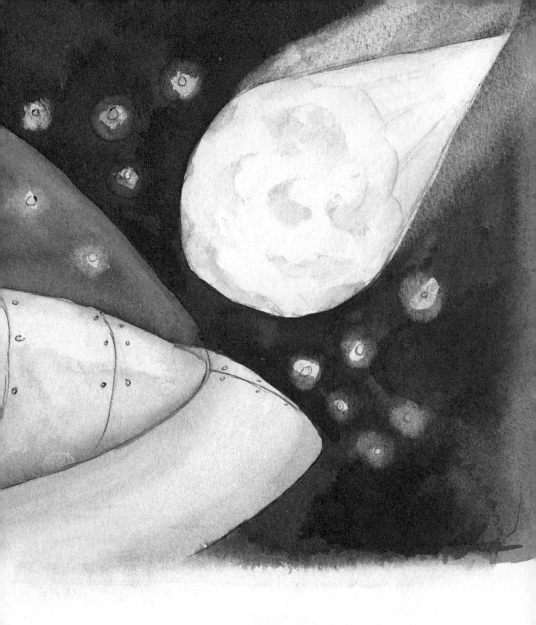

She grabbed the controls and the rocket
swerved away from the comet. It was
just in time. "I picked up your SOS, and
teleported myself here right away,"
Mom said.

13

Mom looked at Zack. "Just wait till I get you home!" she said with an angry frown.

Zack had a feeling that he might be grounded for a very long time. But for once, he didn't mind too much!

Hamster Sleepover

Ali looked out of her bedroom window.
There, at last, were her best friends
coming up the front walk.

Ashley and Martha had sleeping bags
under their arms. Daisy was holding
a big green blanket. They all saw her
and waved.

"This is going to be the best sleepover party ever!" Ali said. She jumped off her bed and ran down the stairs two at a time.

After a dinner of pizza and chocolate cake—everyone's favorite—the girls got ready for bed.

"Ali has never wanted to go to bed *this* early before!" joked her mom.

As the four friends snuggled down for the night in Ali's room, there was a loud scratching noise outside the bedroom door.

"What's that?" asked Daisy.

Then they all heard a loud meow.

"It's Tiger!" said Ali with a grin. Tiger was Ali's cat. "I think she wants to come in and play!"

Martha got out of her sleeping bag. "Should I let her in?" she asked.

But there was a sudden shout from Daisy. "No! Don't open the door!" she said. "Where's Lulu? She isn't in her cage!"

The girls all looked at the hamster cage in the corner of the room. Daisy was right. Ali's hamster, Lulu, was missing.

"Oh no!" said Ali. "We have to find her! Quick!"

The girls began a crazy hunt for Lulu, while Tiger still scratched at the bedroom door.

"Hang on, Tiger!" Ashley called. "You can't come in yet!"

Daisy searched under Ali's bed. Ashley looked through the pile of sleeping bags. Martha checked behind the bookcase. There was no sign of Lulu.

Ali opened a drawer. "Sometimes she likes to sleep in my socks," she said.

But Lulu wasn't there either. "Where can she be?" Ali groaned.

Just then, Martha spotted something. "Look!" she said.

The girls all laughed. They had found Lulu at last, curled up fast asleep in one of Ali's pink slippers.

"She's having her very own sleepover!" Ali said.

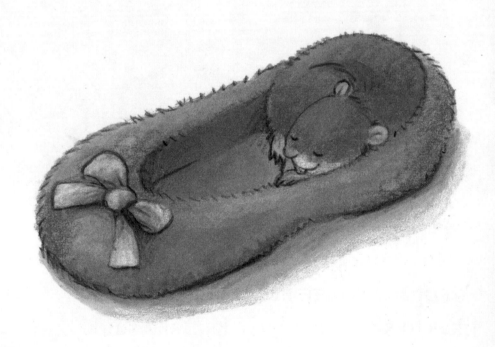

Disappearing Books

It was the hottest summer Molly could remember. The library felt nice and cool as she walked in. She'd come on an errand for her mom.

"I'm looking for a birthday cake cookbook," she told Ms. Brown, the librarian.

Ms. Brown shook her head. "Sorry, Molly. A lot of the books have disappeared." She pointed to a big gap on one of the shelves.

"All the books in the library have disappeared!" said Molly, when she got home.

"Don't worry," said Molly's mom. "It's too hot to bake anyway. I'll buy Dad a birthday cake." She gave Molly a cold drink. "Your friend Tiffany called while you were out. She's invited you over to her house this afternoon."

"Oh, great!" Molly said, forgetting all about the missing library books.

Tiffany lived in a big house called Parker Heights, just outside the village. Her dad was Freddy Parker—he had been a famous rock star a long time ago.

When Molly arrived at Tiffany's house, her dad was complaining about the hot weather.

"I'm melting!" said Freddy, wiping his forehead.

All the doors in the house were open to keep the rooms cool. Molly's eyes widened as she saw that they were wedged open with books.

She opened one. It was a library book. Molly looked around. At least fifty library books were propping open the doors! "Look, Tiffany," she whispered.

Tiffany turned to her dad. "Daddy! You can't take as many books from the library as you want, just because you're rich and famous!" she scolded.

"I guess you're right, Tiff," Freddy said sheepishly. "Let's take the books back."

Freddy, Tiffany and Molly staggered into the library carrying armfuls of books.

"Hey, sorry about borrowing your books without asking," Freddy said to Ms.

Brown. "Why don't you come over to our place for a swim?" He gave Ms. Brown his famous smile.

Ms. Brown was very happy to get her books back but she still made sure that Freddy paid a big library fine for taking the books without signing them out.

She was happy to meet her favorite rock star though. "I'm your number one fan!" she said, her cheeks turning pink.

An hour or so later, Ms. Brown was sipping a cold drink with Freddy, as Molly and Tiffany splashed around in the Parker Heights pool.

"This is the life!" Molly heard her say.

The Shopping Trip

"I wish I could buy a new bike," said Eddie, looking into the bike store window. "Mine's old."

"Me too," said Josh. "But neither of us has any money—and it's not our birthdays for a long time!"

They both sighed.

Eddie grabbed Josh's arm. "I know!" he said. "We could make our own money, running errands and doing odd jobs for people!"

Josh didn't look too sure. "It will take us a long time to earn enough for two bikes," he said.

"We'd better get started, then!" Eddie replied. "Come on!"

"Try Mrs. Cole next door," said Eddie's mom, when the two friends told her their plan. "She might have a few odd jobs you could do."

Mrs. Cole gave Eddie and Josh a huge shopping list. "Make sure you don't forget anything!" she snapped. Mrs. Cole was grumpy.

At the supermarket, Eddie and Josh spent a long time finding everything on the list.

They paid at the checkout and stared at the pile of heavy bags.

"How are we going to carry all this?" Josh asked.

"Wait here!" Eddie told Josh. And he raced off.

He returned with his baby sister's stroller and Rusty, his dog. "Put the groceries in the stroller, Josh," he said, tying Rusty's leash to the stroller. "Rusty can pull the groceries home for us."

"Awesome!" said Josh.

But as Josh put the last bag in the stroller, Rusty spotted a cat and ran after it.

"Quick!" yelled Eddie. "Follow that stroller!"

As Rusty and the stroller passed Mrs. Cole's house, Rusty dodged a lamp post and CRASH! The stroller smashed right into it.

Five big grocery bags flew through the air and then landed with a terrible clatter.

Mrs. Cole rushed out. "Clean up this mess!" she shouted. "And then buy me some more groceries with your own money!" She marched back into her house and slammed the door.

The boys went back to pick up the groceries. This time they carried the bags back themselves.

Mr. Cole paid them and they told him they'd decided not to get dogs to help them with the shopping again!

Egg Raiders

Zac and Lili lived in Canada on Karlin Island. They loved living there. They had lots of fun and had some incredible adventures.

"Do you want to come with me to see the gannets?" Mom asked Zac and Lili one day.

"Yes, please!" they said together.

Gannets were rare sea birds that lived on Black Rock, a small rocky island nearby.

"I hope some of the eggs have hatched," said Lili, as they sailed over to Black Rock. "I can't wait to see the chicks!"

As soon as they had landed, Zac and Lili
ran off to the other side of the island.

Suddenly, Zac grabbed Lili's arm. "Look
at those men!" he said, pointing.

41

Lili looked. "Oh no! They're stealing the gannet eggs!" she gasped.

"We can't let them get away," said Zac. "We have to do something."

Zac started running towards the beach. "If we let their boat go they can't escape. Come on, Lili!" he called.

Lili followed him. They both ran as fast as they could.

They found the thieves' boat, tied up on the beach.

It was difficult to untie the knot but at last they untied it. Lili and Zac watched the boat float away, and then went to tell Mom what was happening.

"Good job," she said, when she heard what they had done. Then she called the coast guard and told him about the thieves.

"I'll be right there," he said. "Leave those thieves to me."

The thieves were looking for their boat when the coast guard arrived.

"You two had better come with me," he said sternly, taking the eggs from them.

When the gannets saw the men being taken away, they started making loud calls.

"I think they're happy the men are gone!" said Lili.

"Or maybe they're saying thank you— to you!" said Mom.

Troublesome Tina

It was Saturday morning. Zack's little sister was late for her moon-dancing class.

"Hurry up, Zelda!" said Mom. "It's time to go!" She went to get Zelda's space suit and found Zack's lying on the floor.

47

"Your space suit is dirty, Zack. Can you wash it please?" Mom shouted, as she rushed out of the house with Zelda.

Zack looked at his space suit. His favorite intergalactic TV show was on in five minutes, and he really didn't feel like washing it. Then he had an idea.

Zack gave Tina the House Robot his space suit, and pressed "wash" on her control panel.

Immediately Tina started washing the suit. It was all so easy. Zack went to watch his favorite TV shows on the couch. He soon fell asleep.

49

Zack woke feeling uncomfortable. He was sitting in a puddle of water. Tina had washed his space suit, but she hadn't stopped there. She had washed the whole house from top to bottom, and everything was covered in soap bubbles. What a huge mess!

Zack looked at his watch. Mom would be back soon. In a panic, he pushed Tina's "power dry" setting, and switched her speed up to "very fast."

Tina whizzed around as fast as her
wheels would spin, drying everything in
sight with blasts of hot air.

The front door opened. Mom and Zelda
were home. Zack pushed Tina into the
kitchen and ran to meet them.

Mom was holding something shiny in her
hand. "What *have* you done to your space
suit?" she asked. Tina's hot air had shrunk
Zack's space suit to half its size.

"I should send you to your room without dinner," said Mom, "but I won't, because you have cleaned the house so well!"

Zack started to tell her that Tina had done it all, then changed his mind. "No problem," he smiled.

Truth or Dare?

Martha was having a sleepover with her friends at Martha's house. They were playing a game of "Truth or Dare?"

"I dare you to sneak downstairs and get us some ice cream," Martha said to Ashley.

"You're on!" Ashley grinned.
She climbed out of her sleeping bag
and opened the bedroom door.
The house was very quiet as she
crept downstairs.

In the kitchen, Ashley opened the
freezer and took out a large tub of
ice cream. She pulled off the lid.
Double-chocolate chip—yummy!

As she grabbed four spoons from the drawer, Martha's dog Benny appeared. "Woof!" he barked.

"Shh! Benny!" Ashley whispered. "Be quiet!" But it was too late. Ashley heard a bedroom door opening and footsteps on the stairs.

She dashed behind the kitchen door just in time to hear Martha's dad grabbing something from the umbrella stand. "I'm armed!" he shouted.

Ashley's heart raced. Benny barked again. How was she going to get back upstairs without being caught?

She waited until Martha's dad went into the dining room and then hurried into the hall. As she raced towards the stairs, the hall rug slipped. Ashley skidded backwards, the ice cream and spoons flying into the air.

The spoons crashed to the wooden floor
with a loud clatter—and the ice cream
tub landed on Ashley.

Double-chocolate chip ice cream dripped down Ashley's face. With his tail wagging quickly, Benny came over to help clean up.

Ashley looked up to see Martha's dad grinning down at her. Martha, Daisy and Ali were giggling on the stairs.

"At least it wasn't a burglar," said Martha's dad, putting his large blue umbrella back into its stand.

Ashley took off her icy hat and shivered. "I don't want any ice cream now," she said. "I think I'd rather have a hot shower!"

Disgusting Donuts

"One donut, please," Molly said.
She handed her money to Mr. Jones,
the baker. Mr. Jones made the best donuts
ever.

Molly sat down on a bench outside the bakery. She took a great big bite out of her donut. "Yuck!" she said, spitting it out. It tasted disgusting.

Tiffany and Carlos, another of Molly's school friends, walked by. "You're eating one of Mr. Jones's donuts, aren't you?" Carlos asked. "They used to be tasty, but not any more. We've stopped buying them."

"I don't blame you," said Molly, throwing the rest of her donut in the trash can. She heard giggling and turned around. It was John and Jamie, Mr. Jones's bratty twin sons.

"What's so funny?" Molly asked angrily.

"Nothing," they said. They ran back into the bakery, still giggling.

"I wonder if the twins are somehow behind the disgusting donuts?" said Molly thoughtfully.

"I bet they are!" Tiffany replied. "Do you remember when they watered down all the glue at school so it wouldn't stick?"

"Let's find out!" said Carlos.

The three friends sneaked into the bakery. John and Jamie were in the kitchen.

"Look what they're doing!" whispered Molly. John and Jamie were pouring salt into their dad's sugar shaker.

So this was what had happened to Mr. Jones's donuts! He was sweetening them with salt instead of sugar, and it was all the twins' fault.

Molly grabbed John and Jamie and dragged them into the bakery. John was still holding the sugar shaker. Jamie was pretending to cry.

"Look what John and Jamie have been doing, Mr. Jones!" said Molly. "They've been ruining your donuts."

Mr. Jones was very angry with John and Jamie. "You two can spend the weekend doing dishes in the kitchen," he said to them.

Then he turned to Molly, Tiffany, and Carlos. "Thank you so much!" he said. "You can each take home a free box of cakes for your families." He smiled. "But I'll understand if you don't want donuts!"

Car Wash

Eddie's dad was washing his car.

"I really hate this job!" he said to Eddie and Josh. "If you want to earn some money, you should wash people's cars."

71

"You can use our driveway," he said.

Eddie and Josh thought this was a great idea. They made a big sign, filled some buckets with soapy water, and borrowed some sponges.

Soon afterwards, Mr. Cole drove in. "Hello boys," he said. "I'll be your first customer!"

CAR WASH - $1 A CAR!

Eddie and Josh looked at the car. It was very dirty!

"This is going to take us so long!" said Eddie.

Melinda, who lived down the road, was walking by.

"Hello, Melinda!" Eddie and Josh called, holding up their soapy sponges.

"What are you doing?" asked Melinda. "That looks like fun!"

Eddie had an idea. "It *is* fun!" he lied.
"If you give us $1, you can help."

"Thank you!" said Melinda, looking
pleased. "I don't have the money, but
I'll ask my dad for it later."

Eddie handed Melinda a sponge and did
a high five with Josh behind her back.

Melinda was a hard worker,
and soon the car was
sparkling clean.

"You've done a great job, boys!" said Mr. Cole. "Thank you."

Melinda's dad was the next person to pull into the driveway.

"Hello, Dad!" said Melinda. "Do you want us to wash your car?"

Eddie pointed to the sign. "It'll cost $1," he said. Melinda's dad got out his wallet.

"Can I have $1 too, Dad?" asked Melinda. "I need to pay Eddie and Josh for letting me help."

CAR
WASH
- $1 A CAR!

Her dad put the wallet back in his pocket. "You'll do nothing of the sort!" he replied, angrily.

He turned to Eddie and Josh. "I'm going to talk to your parents!" he said.

Eddie and Josh's parents were not happy! "You two can wash Melinda's dad's car for free," said Josh's mom.

"Then you can wash our cars for free," added Eddie's mom.

Eddie and Josh sighed.

"Can I help for free?" asked Melinda. "I love washing cars!"

Man Overboard!

Zac and Lili had been to the mainland with Dad to get supplies. They boarded the ferry to sail home to Karlin Island.

Dad found a friend to talk to so Zac and Lili went to look around.

"Be careful," Dad shouted after them.

"We will," they promised.

Zac and Lili headed up to the deck so they could look out for seals.

"Look at that little boy, Zac," Lili gasped, pointing. "That's so dangerous."

A little boy was sitting on the top of the ferry railing.

Suddenly, the ferry hit a large wave and tipped to the side. The boy slipped and fell into the ocean.

Lili and Zac rushed over to the rail.

"Help!" the boy shouted, waving his arms. "I can't swim!"

"I'll throw him the life preserver," Zac told Lili. "You go and tell the captain to stop the ferry."

"Hold on!" Zac called. "Lili's gone to get help. You'll be out of there soon."
Zac knew it was important for the boy to stay calm.

The ferry stopped moving. Zac smiled. Fast work, Lili!

The captain came hurrying over, with Lili, Dad, and the boy's worried parents.

"I'll lower the lifeboat," the captain said.

Dad offered to row the lifeboat.

"Be careful, Dad!" cried Lili anxiously.
"The waves are really big!"

Dad rowed carefully out to the boy and
pulled him into the lifeboat.

Before long the boy was back on board, wrapped in a blanket.

"Thank you for saving me," the boy said to Lili and Zac. "I'll never sit on the railing again!"

Lost Boots

Zack really wanted to get into the Space School powerball team. He had begged Mom to buy him some brand-new jet boots, and he practiced all weekend before try outs.

But on the morning of the try outs, Zack's new jet boots weren't in his locker.

The old pair he borrowed were too big for him. During the warm-up Zack tripped and landed on his back. He knew he would never make the team.

Zack limped off the court sadly, but
Coach Cooper stopped him.

"I know how much you want to be on this
team, Zack," he said. "So I'm going to
put you on the junior team. Don't worry,
your time will come."

At the game Zack sat on the bench, watching his team warm up.

"See how a *real* player does it!" said Baz, the team captain. He fired a powerball straight at Zack.

"Baz, I saw that," said Coach Cooper. "You're off my team."

"It's a stupid game, anyway!" shouted Baz. He stormed out, kicking off his jet boots.

Zack looked at the jet boots. They were just like his lost boots… In fact, they _were_ his boots. Baz must have stolen them!

"Your turn, Zack!" said Coach Cooper. Zack couldn't believe his luck. He was in the powerball team.

The game began. Both teams were scoring well. Every player wanted to win. With a minute to go, Zack's team were trailing by one point. Zack switched his boots to turbo charge and jumped into the air. He slammed the ball at the backboard, and it dropped neatly through the basket.

The buzzer sounded. Zack's team were the champions. Zack had won the game!

"Good job, Zack," said Coach Cooper. "We've never won the trophy before!" Everyone cheered.

Surprise Sleepover

It was the week before Daisy's birthday
and it had been snowing all day. She
was with her friends at Ashley's house.
Though it was still afternoon, it was
growing dark already.

"What do you want for your birthday, Daisy?" Ashley asked her.

"I'd love a dog!" said Daisy. "One like Benny," she added, smiling at Martha.

"Me too!" said Ali. "But I don't think Tiger would be very happy about it!"

Suddenly the light in Ashley's room went out, and everything became very, very dark.

"What's happening?" yelled Ali. The girls grabbed each other's hands in the dark.

Daisy stepped back and fell over a chair. "Ouch!" she moaned.

"Let's go downstairs," said Ashley.

They stumbled forward and Ashley felt for the door handle. Finding it, she pulled the door open and the others followed her into the hall.

The light had gone out there too. It was as black as night.

"Mom!" Ashley shouted.

Ashley's mom came up the stairs holding a candle. "Don't worry, girls, it's just a black out!" she said. "Come on, we'll make ourselves cozy in the living room."

Downstairs in the living room, Ashley's dad was building a fire in the fireplace. The girls looked through the curtains and saw that all the windows in the street were dark.

"The snow's knocked out the power," Ashley's dad said. "And the roads are all blocked."

"But how will we get home?" Ali asked.

Ashley's mom told them not to worry and went to call their parents.

Martha's teeth began to chatter. "It's so cold!" she said.

Ashley's dad went to get some blankets. "Here, girls," he said. "These will keep you warm until the fire gets going."

The girls snuggled up on the two couches and watched as the fire began to crackle to life.

Ashley's mom came in a little later with some mugs of hot chocolate. "I've got a surprise, girls!" she said. "Guess what?"

"What, Mom?" asked Ashley.

"You're all going to stay here tonight because of the snow!" she said with a smile. "You're having a surprise sleepover!"

"Yay!" they all cheered.

"Snowstorms are great!" said Martha.

Ghost in the Attic

Molly was doing her homework with Carlos one evening when there was a knock on the front door. It was Mrs. Dimley, the next-door neighbor. She looked rather scared.

"Is something wrong?" asked Molly's mom.

"It's silly really, but I think my house is haunted!" Mrs. Dimley replied.

Molly grew excited. She loved ghost stories.

"At night, I can hear bumping, tapping, and rustling noises coming from my attic," explained Mrs. Dimley.

Molly's mom made Mrs. Dimley a cup of coffee, and Mrs. Dimley said she felt better.

But the next morning, when Molly and Carlos were helping Molly's dad in the

yard, Mrs. Dimley came back looking
upset. "My lights aren't working now,
and the TV keeps going on and off," she
said. "Something's wrong. If this doesn't
stop, I'll have to move out!"

Molly liked old Mrs. Dimley, and didn't want her to leave. It was time to find out what was making her so unhappy.

"Mom, can we borrow a flashlight?" she asked. "We're going next door to look in Mrs. Dimley's attic."

"I'll come with you," said her dad.

In Mrs. Dimley's living room, Molly's dad shivered as a bump came from the attic and the television flickered. "I don't like this at all, Molly," he said.

"Don't be silly, Dad!" said Molly.

Molly's dad helped her and Carlos up
into Mrs. Dimley's attic. When Molly
switched on her flashlight, she couldn't
believe her eyes. What a
mess! There were shredded
newspapers everywhere.

Hiding in a corner was a family of frightened squirrels.

"Dad!" called Molly. "Look what we've found!" Her dad climbed up the ladder and looked into the attic. "Those squirrels must have gotten in through that hole in the roof," he chuckled. "They've chewed through lots of wires. No wonder Mrs. Dimley's electricity isn't working right!"

Carlos ran next door to tell Mrs. Dimley the news.

"Thank goodness for that!" she said.
She called a vet, who came around
right away.

"I'll take your squirrels to the local park,"
he said. "They'll be much happier living
there."

"And I'll fix the hole in your roof," said Molly's dad. "Then you won't have any more unwelcome visitors."

Mrs. Dimley was pleased. "You're all so kind," she said. She gave Molly and Carlos a big hug. "And you two are very smart kids!"

Yard Makeover

Josh's mom was doing some gardening. It gave Josh an idea.

He hurried over to Eddie's. "Let's see if anyone will pay us to do some gardening," he suggested.

Mr. Peacock across the street was happy to be asked. "I'll pay you to mow the lawn and do some weeding," he said. "The lawn mower is in the garage."

"My turn first!" said Eddie, starting up the engine.

It wasn't easy to steer the mower in a straight line. "Oops!" Eddie muttered, as he plowed through a flowerbed.

Josh began to pull up weeds. "Oops!" he said, as each weed turned out to be a carrot.

Mr. Peacock came hurrying down the path. He looked very upset.

"My beautiful flowers!" he cried. "And my prize carrots!"

"We're sorry, Mr. Peacock," said Josh.

"We're not very good at gardening," Eddie added.

With a sigh, Mr. Peacock bent down to inspect the damage to his carrots. He picked up something shiny from the dug-up soil.

"What's this?" he asked. And then he gasped. "It's an old rare coin!" he said. "Quick boys, get digging—see if you can find any more!"

Together, Josh, Eddie and Mr. Peacock dug up a whole mound of rare coins.

"My mom runs the store at the local museum," said Eddie. "She says that there is a woman there who knows all there is to know about rare coins."

"Let's take them down there!" said Mr. Peacock.

The woman at the museum was very
excited when she saw the coins. "These
are very rare!" she said.

She looked at Mr. Peacock. "And they're
probably very valuable!"

Back home, Mr. Peacock showed Josh and Eddie how to do the gardening properly. They worked hard all afternoon and then Mr. Peacock paid them.

"I think you've given us too much money, Mr. Peacock," said Eddie.

"No I haven't," he said. "It's to say thank you for helping me find the coins too."

Beach Rescue

Zac and Lili were worried. They hadn't
seen their favorite dolphin, Whistler,
for a while.

"Dolphins sometimes swim far out in the ocean," Mom told them. "I'm sure Whistler will be back soon."

But there was no sign of Whistler the next day. Or the next.

"What if something has happened to him?" said Lili.

"Can we go and look for him, Dad?" begged Zac.

"Okay," Dad agreed. "But I'm sure he's fine."

They all set off in Dad's boat.

After a while, they saw some dolphins ahead. "Let's get a little closer and see if Whistler is among them," said Dad. But Whistler was nowhere to be seen.

Now Lili and Zac were really worried.
Where was Whistler?

To their surprise the dolphins started to
swim around the boat. They whistled
and leaped in the air. They swam away
for a bit and then came back again.

"I think they want us to follow them, Dad!" said Zac.

"You may be right!" agreed Dad.

The dolphins led them to a nearby island. As they got closer, Lili saw another dolphin lying on the beach. "It's Whistler!" she shouted. "He must be hurt!"

Dad tied up the boat and they all ran over to Whistler.

"What happened to him?" asked Zac.

"He must have swam too close to the island, then got stranded when the tide went out," Dad explained. "If we don't get him back into the ocean soon, he will die," he added quietly.

"Oh no!" cried Lili and Zac.

Dad took out his cell phone and called Dolphin Rescue. He told them all about Whistler. Then he turned to Lili and Zac.

"We must keep Whistler wet until
Dolphin Rescue arrive," he said.

They got buckets from the boat and
began pouring ocean water over
Whistler.

125

At last, Dolphin Rescue arrived and Whistler was helped back into the ocean.

The dolphin swam off and then leaped out of the water and clicked happily.

"I think he's saying thank you!" laughed Dad.

Henry's Visit

Zack was excited. His pen pal Henry was coming to visit, all the way from Planet Yopp. Zack and Henry kept in touch by satellite text, but today they were going to meet for the first time.

When Henry arrived, Zack couldn't believe his eyes. It wasn't Henry's bright-green scaly skin that surprised him, but his two heads and seven wavy tentacles.

"Bopp, gloppy dopp!" said Henry cheerfully.

Zack looked at his dad. "What did he say?" he asked.

"You've forgotten to turn on your translator, silly," said Dad. He switched the control on Zack's suit to "on."

"Hello, Zack," said Henry.

Zack could understand him now. "Hello, Henry," he replied.

It was hard finding things to do with
Henry. Zack took him roller-skating,
but there weren't enough roller skates in
Henry's size. They tried moon dancing,
but Henry tripped everyone.

In the end, they decided to go for lunch
at Zack's favorite restaurant, the Moon
Rock Café.

Henry ate more food than Zack would eat in a week. He gobbled up ten cosmic burgers, eight plates of meteor fries, and six galactic fruit salads.

"Yummy!" said Henry.

Zack wasn't so happy. He didn't have enough money left to pay for the enormous meal.

When he found out, the restaurant manager wasn't happy. "You can do the dishes!" he said.

In the kitchen, Henry washed the dirty
plates, spinning and juggling them
with his tentacles. Zack could hardly
believe his eyes! In just a few minutes
they had finished.

The manager was amazed. "You can both have vacation jobs if you want!" he said.

Zack and Henry were thrilled. They were going to get paid and have a great vacation too.

Pajama Party

It was school vacation. Ali, Martha, and Ashley were at Daisy's for a sleepover.

"Let's have a dance!" said Daisy as they munched on some chips. "We can try out the disco ball lamp I got for my birthday."

"Great idea!" said the others.

Daisy got out her best music for dancing to, and the others looked through Daisy's closet for party clothes they could all wear.

Once they had all changed, the girls made a space on Daisy's bedroom floor and closed the curtains. Daisy put on the music and Ashley turned on the new party ball lamp.

All at once the room was filled with
music and sparkling lights, just like a
real party!

The girls started to sing and dance. Daisy picked up her hairbrush and jumped onto her bed. "Look at me!" she laughed. "I could be a rock star—it's easy!" Her friends cheered as she sang along, pretending the hairbrush was a microphone.

Before long, Ashley, Ali, and Martha were singing and dancing on the bed too.

Just as Ali was in the middle of a high kick there was a loud cracking noise and Daisy's bed collapsed. Martha and Ashley landed on the floor in a heap, and Ali tripped forwards and crashed into Daisy.

Daisy's big brother Jon came rushing
into the room. "What's going on in
here?" he grinned. "Disco dancing
accident?"

"It's not funny!" said Daisy, rubbing her head. "We've broken the bed!"

"I could fix it," said Jon. "I might not even tell Mom. What's it worth?"

The girls looked at each other. "How about half a bar of chocolate?" said Martha.

Jon laughed. "No way! You'll have to do better than that!" he said.

In the end the girls had to promise Jon *all* their candy and potato chips before he went to get the toolbox.

When Jon had fixed the bed the girls got into their pajamas.

"The next time I'm dancing, it's going to be on a real dance floor!" groaned Daisy.

"Or a stage!" laughed Ashley.

Stolen Necklace

"Happy birthday, Tiffany!" Molly said, hugging her friend. She had been looking forward to Tiffany's birthday party for weeks.

The party began with a magic show in the yard. Everyone was amazed at the magician's tricks.

But then suddenly, Tiffany's mom, Tracy, ran onto the stage. "Stop the show!" she cried. "I can't find my diamond necklace! It's been stolen!"

144

"Your diamond necklace?" asked Tiffany's dad worriedly.

"Yes—and it's worth a fortune!" said Tiffany's mom. "Call the police!"

"Mommy's always losing her jewels and panicking," said Tiffany angrily. "I bet it's not stolen at all. And it's ruined my birthday party!"

Molly wanted to help Tiffany. And she liked mysteries even more than magic shows!

"I might just, um, go to the bathroom, Tiff," she said, standing up.

"Let's do some investigating!" she said
to herself.

On the way up to the house, Molly
heard a scream behind a bush, and
hurried to see what had happened.

She found Tiffany's two little sisters
in their play house, having an argument.
They were dressed as princesses.

"It's mine! Give it back!" said Zara.

"No, I got it first!" said Trixie. She was waving a sparkly necklace in the air. "Hello, you two," said Molly. "Where did you get that pretty necklace?"

"We borrowed it," said Trixie.

"To play princesses," said Zara.

Molly laughed. "I think we'd better tell your mom," she said.

Tiffany's mom was very happy to have her necklace back. "Next time, just ask before you borrow my things," she said, giving Zara and Trixie a hug. "Now let's find Tiffany and get this magic show started again!"

After the magic show was over, Tiffany's
mom made another announcement.
"Good news!" she cried. "My necklace
has been found. And to celebrate,
all the girls are invited to try on my
jewelry collection."

Tiffany clapped excitedly. "This is
going to be great—come on, everyone!"
she said.

As her party guests admired themselves in the huge dressing-room mirror, Tiffany thanked her mom.

"It's Molly you need to thank, Tiff," Tiffany's mom said with a smile. "She's the one who saved the day!"

Fat Cat

Eddie and Josh had set up a pet-sitting service. Their first job was to feed Fluffy, Mr. and Mrs. Cole's cat, while they went on vacation for a week.

"Don't forget, Fluffy needs to be fed three times a day," Mrs. Cole told the boys, as she handed over the huge cat.

When Mrs. Cole was in the car, Mr. Cole turned to Eddie and Josh. "Try not to let Fluffy eat too much!" he whispered. "And make sure she gets some exercise. See you next week."

"Mr. Cole is right," said Josh a week later, as he and Eddie watched Fluffy start on her twenty-first bowl of food. "Fluffy definitely eats too much and exercises too little."

"Let's see if we can help," said Eddie. He made a barking noise, like a dog.

Eddie and Josh had never seen a cat move so fast. She bolted through the cat door into the back yard and bolted up the nearest tree.

Josh and Eddie ran outside.

"Here, Fluffy!" Josh called. But Fluffy wouldn't come down.

"Now look what you've done, Eddie!" said Josh.

"Don't worry, I'll get her down," said Eddie. He went home to get his toy bow and arrow and a rope. Then he tied the rope to one of the arrows and fired it over a branch.

"Hold one end of the rope, Josh," Eddie said. Slowly, Eddie pulled himself up the tree using the rope. "Phew! This is hard work!" he panted.

But just as Eddie reached the branch that Fluffy sat on, the cat scampered back down the tree trunk all by herself.

Eddie looked down. "Oh no!" he cried. "*I'm* stuck now!"

"It looks like we arrived home just in time!" said Mr. Cole, walking into the yard. He put a ladder against the tree and helped Eddie down. "What were you doing up there?" he asked.

Eddie and Josh explained, and Mr. Cole laughed.

When Mrs. Cole came outside she didn't find it quite so funny. "Fluffy doesn't usually climb trees," she said, cuddling the enormous cat and frowning at Eddie and Josh.

Fluffy purred and looked smug.

"Well she should probably climb them more often," said Mr. Cole.

He turned to Josh and Eddie. "Thanks for giving Fluffy some exercise!" he said giving them their money. "Perhaps I'll start barking at her, too!" he joked.

Stranded

Dad had to check on some seal pups near Black Rock, so Lili and Zac went with him.

"They're so cute," said Lili, smiling.

"They're all happy and healthy too," said Dad, looking pleased.

They set off home, but they hadn't gone very far when Zac noticed water swishing around his feet. "Dad! The boat's leaking!" he shouted.

Lili looked. "The water's coming in fast, too!" she gasped. "It must be a big hole!"

Dad quickly fetched a bucket. "Let's try to bail the water out," he said. "I'll head back to Black Rock."

But the water was coming in too fast. Soon it was almost up to Lili's knees.

"Dad! The boat's sinking!" she cried.

"Don't worry. Look, we're almost there," said Dad, pointing to the rocky island not far ahead. "We can swim the rest of the way."

They jumped overboard in their life jackets, and swam through the ocean.

"I'll call for help," Dad said when they were safely on Black Rock. But his cell phone had disappeared.
"Oh no! It must have fallen out of my pocket into the ocean," he groaned.

Lili and Zac were cold, wet, and miserable. They wanted to go home!

"Don't worry, Mom will come looking for us soon," Dad told them.

"But how will she know where to find us?" asked Lili.

Dad thought about that. "We'll light a fire," he decided. "When Mom sees the smoke she'll come to find out what's going on."

They collected some dry branches and twigs, and Dad rubbed two twigs together to spark the fire to life.

They all huddled around the fire to
keep warm.

Before long Lili spotted a motorboat
chugging towards them. It was the coast
guard.

Then they heard a familiar voice coming through the coast guard's megaphone. It was Mom!

"Need some help over there?" she asked.

"Hooray!" cheered Zac.

"We'll soon be home now," said Dad.

Zack's Birthday

Zack woke up early. He had been waiting for this day for weeks, and now it was here at last. It was his birthday!

Zack couldn't wait to open all his presents. He hoped one of them was the latest CD by Alan and the Aliens, his favorite band.

He jumped out of bed and ran downstairs. Mom was in the kitchen, oiling Tina the House Robot.

"Hello, Zack," said Mom. "Could you set the table for breakfast, please? Tina's not working this morning."

Zack couldn't believe his ears. "No Happy Birthday? Where's Dad?" he asked.

"He had to go to work early," said Mom. "He's got a busy day."

Zelda ran into the kitchen. "I've got a school trip today!" she said. "My teacher told us to get to school early, because the space bus leaves at eight o'clock."

"We'd better hurry!" said Mom. She handed Zack a carton of milk. "Get your own breakfast, Zack," she said. "I've got to take Zelda to school."

They had all forgotten his birthday!

Things didn't get better at Space School.
Zack had all his worst classes.

At home time, Zack's best friend
Spud tried to cheer him up.
"I'll race you!" he said. They bounced
home on their space hoppers.

Dad opened the front door. "Surprise!"
he said. All Zack's family were there.
Balloons were everywhere, and there was
a huge pile of presents.

"We didn't really forget," said Mom,
giving Zack a kiss. "Go on, birthday boy,
open your presents!"

Zack ripped open an envelope. "It's tickets to see Alan and the Aliens at the Moondust Superdrome tonight!" he cried.

"We're all going—Spud too," said Dad.

Zack grinned. This was going to be a fantastic birthday after all!

Birthday Sleepover

It was Ali's birthday and she had
invited her friends to a special
sleepover. Since it was a warm summer
evening, they were going to camp in
the backyard in Ali's new tent. They had
been looking forward to it for weeks and
were planning a special midnight feast.

The moon was shining brightly as the girls settled into the tent. Ali, Martha, and Daisy zipped up the flap and climbed into their sleeping bags.

"It's too bad Ashley couldn't come," said Martha. "This is going to be so much fun!"

They unpacked their feast of potato
chips, cookies, and peanut butter and
jelly sandwiches. As they were eating,
they made each other laugh with spooky
ghost stories.

Daisy began telling them about an old barn nearby. Her brother had said it was haunted.

Then there was a bang from outside the tent.

"What was that?" asked Martha, looking worried.

"Just a cat, or something," said Ali, nervously.

They all listened again. There was another bang and then a noise that sounded like a twig snapping.

Martha jumped. "That wasn't a cat!" she said, grabbing her flashlight.

"What's that strange rustling noise?" said Daisy. "It's coming from right outside!"

Ali reached for her shoes. "I don't like this at all!" she said.

Martha and Daisy scrambled out of their sleeping bags.

"Let's get out of here!" yelled Daisy.

The girls grabbed their things and squeezed out of the tent.

"Quick! Follow me!" shouted Ali. She began to lead them across the grass towards the house.

"Wait!" said a voice behind them. "Where are you all going?"

It was Ashley!

"My mom said I could come after all!" she laughed. "But it was hard to find your tent in the dark."

Ali, Daisy, and Martha laughed. "So it was you making all those noises!" said Daisy. "Not a ghost at all!"

Ali hugged Ashley. "I'm so glad you're here," she said. "It wouldn't have been a real birthday without you."

"Now let's finish off this midnight feast!" cried Martha.

Crop Circles

Molly's dad was reading the newspaper. "Look at this!" he said, showing Molly a photo of some huge circles of flattened corn in Farmer Gilbert's cornfield.

"How did they get there?" asked Molly.

"No one knows, but some people say they were made by aliens," her dad replied, with a smile. "Perhaps a UFO landed on the cornfield one night!"

Molly couldn't stop thinking about the crop circles. She didn't believe they were made by aliens. It was a mystery, and she wanted to solve it.

By dinner time, she had come up with a plan. "Carlos and I have to do a bat-watch project," she told her dad. "Would you come out with us one night to count bats? I thought we could go up to Farmer Gilbert's cornfield."

Her dad smiled. "OK," he agreed. "Since there's no school tomorrow, we'll go tonight."

They took a thermos of hot chocolate
with them up to the cornfield. The moon
was shining brightly, and stars twinkled
in the sky. The three of them found a
good place to sit at the top of the hill.

185

It was getting late, and Molly felt tired. Her dad snored beside her. Molly's own eyes began to close—and then she opened them wide again as she saw something move in the corn. She had almost missed it! Two teenage boys were creeping into the field.

Molly nudged her dad and Carlos. "Look over there!" she said.

Molly's dad woke with a start.

The boys started beating down the corn with their skateboards. They moved quickly to make a big circle.

Molly, Carlos, and her dad walked over to them. "You stop that right now!" her dad said.

The boys looked embarrassed. "We were only having a little fun," the boys replied. "We like reading about our crop circles in the newspaper."

"If you promise you won't do this again, we won't tell on you," Molly said.

"It's a deal," the boys said, looking relieved.

Next week, Molly ran to the local store to buy the newspaper as soon as it came out.

"Look, Dad!" Molly showed him the latest photo of Farmer Gilbert's field. "No more crop circles. It says the aliens have left!"

Her dad smiled. "But we know the truth, don't we?" he said.

The Work of Art

Eddie had a great idea. "We could put a poster on the school bulletinboard," he said. "Eddie and Josh's Odd Job Service—No job too big or too small."

"Let's do it!" said Josh.

On Friday afternoon, Ms. Price, the principal of the preschool next door, called the boys into her office. "I saw your poster," she told them. "I have a job for you: I'd like you to paint the preschool playground wall."

"Do you mean that old wall in the corner?" asked Josh.

"Yes," said Ms. Price. "It needs brightening up."

"When should we start?" asked Josh.

"Tomorrow after school," said Ms. Price.

After school the next day, the janitor carried some paint cans and paintbrushes into the playground.

"Ms. Price didn't say what color she wanted the wall to be painted," the janitor said, opening the cans of paint. "I'll let you choose." Then he went back into his garage at the side of the playground.

Eddie and Josh looked at the paints. There was red, yellow, green, and purple paint.

"Painting the wall all one color is boring," said Eddie. "We should use all the colors to paint a huge picture."

Josh nodded. "Let's paint some basketball players," he suggested, picking up a can of green paint.

"No, some monsters," said Eddie, taking a can of purple paint.

"Basketball players!" said Josh.

"Monsters!" argued Eddie. He flicked some purple paint at the wall.

"*Basketball players!*" yelled Josh, flicking some green paint over Eddie's purple paint.

By the time Josh and Eddie had finished arguing, the whole wall was splattered with purple and green, and there wasn't a monster or basketball player in sight.

"Oh no!" said Josh, staring at the wall.

"*Now* we're in trouble," said Eddie.

They left the paint cans and ran home.

First thing on Monday morning, Josh and Eddie were called in to see Ms. Price. She was quiet for a moment. Then she clapped her hands in delight. "Great job!" she said. "What a beautiful piece of modern art!"

Eddie and Josh smiled at each other as Ms. Price handed them an envelope. "Here's your money for a job well done!" she said.

The Storm

One night, Lili and Zac were woken up by a big storm. Thunder crashed and lightning flashed. It sounded very scary.

"I can't sleep," said Zac, opening the curtains to look at the storm.

"Me neither," said Lili.

They both went downstairs. Mom and Dad were in the kitchen.

"The storm woke us up," said Zac.

"It's a bad one," agreed Mom.

Suddenly the lights went out.

"The power went out!" cried Lili.

Dad went to get some oil lamps.

They all sat drinking hot chocolate by lamplight and listening to the storm. Then Dad's phone rang. He looked very worried as he talked.

"That was the lighthouse keeper," he said. "The lighthouse has been struck by lightning. Now it doesn't work."

Dad told them that a boat was trying to come into the harbor. "It won't be able to see its way without the light from the lighthouse," he said. "We'll all have to take some searchlights and guide it safely in."

They all made their way to the dark harbor, carrying searchlights.

"First we need to find the boat," said Dad. He shined his big searchlight out toward the ocean. "There it is!" he pointed.

"Oh no!" gasped Mom. "It looks like it's heading for the rocks!"

If the boat hit the rocks it would crash and sink.

They all stood together and shined the searchlights to guide the boat into the harbor. But the boat didn't change direction.

"It's still heading for the rocks!"
shouted Zac.

They watched the boat in fear.
Would it see their lights in time? The boat
got closer and closer to the rocks. Dad
looked very worried.

Then slowly, the boat started to turn
around.

"It must have seen us!" Lili yelled
excitedly.

The boat followed the searchlights safely into the harbor.

When the captain got out, he came over to them. "Thank you so much," he said. "I don't know what would have happened if you weren't here."

"No problem!" said Lili proudly.

Space School Star

As soon as he woke up, Zack knew something was wrong. He looked at his clock—it was nine o'clock! Today was the day of his junior astronaut test, and he should have been at school fifteen minutes ago.

He stumbled out of bed and bumped into Dad on the way to the bathroom.

Dad made a face. "Mom left early this morning, and my alarm clock didn't go off," he complained.

"I'm late for my test!" said Zack.

"And I'm late for work!" replied Dad. "You'll have to get yourself to school today."

Zack got his hover boots. He could fly really fast in them. But then he remembered, they needed new batteries…

Zack wasn't allowed to use the teleporting machine, but he decided this was an emergency. He pressed the buttons carefully to key in his destination. If he made a mistake, he could end up in another galaxy.

Taking a deep breath, he stepped in. Zack shut his eyes and pressed "GO."

Seconds later, he was in the exam room. He had done it!

"Sit down, Zack," said his teacher, Mr. Satellite. "The test is about to begin. Good luck!"

When Zack got home, Mom looked furious. "I found your helmet in the teleporting machine," she said. "What have you been up to, Zack? That is a *very* dangerous machine."

Then the satellite phone rang. Still frowning at Zack, Mom answered it.

When she ended the call Mom went
over to Zack. To his surprise, she gave
him a hug. "That was your teacher,"
she said. "You got an A on your
test today!"

Zack couldn't believe his ears. "Wow!"
he said.

"So I guess I'll let it slide about the teleporting machine," Mom said with a smile. She gave Zack his space helmet. "You'll be a great astronaut one day, Zack, but it seems you're a pretty good one already!"

Sleepover Splash

In Ashley's bedroom Martha and Daisy were rolling out their sleeping bags for another sleepover. Ali was feeding some fruit to Ashley's gerbil, Magic.

"Max is driving me crazy!" said Ashley. "I hate having a twin brother!"

All day long Max had been playing practical jokes on Ashley. He and his friend James had put a frog in her bed and spread mustard in her peanut butter sandwiches. They had also hidden her ballet shoes so she was late for her class.

"Why don't you get back at him?" said Daisy. She sat down on Ashley's bed. "Let's come up with a really good practical joke to play on him!"

Martha and Ali agreed. They all thought for a moment.

"I know!" said Daisy. "Here's a good one! Let's put a bucket of water above his door. When he opens it he'll get soaked!"

"That's a great idea!" said Ashley, jumping up. "I'll go and get a bucket from downstairs and you all make sure Max is out of his room!"

Martha and Ali went out onto the landing and knocked on Max's door.

There was no answer. "All clear!" they called. Ashley came back up with the bucket, and she and Daisy took it to the bathroom to fill it with water.

219

Ashley, Ali, and Martha lifted up the
bucket and handed it to Daisy.

Ashley opened Max's door just enough
so the bucket would balance on top.
"Max!" she called. "There's something in
your room for you!"

Ashley, Ali, and Martha raced across the
hall, back to Ashley's bedroom.

"Hurry, Daisy!" hissed Ashley.

But just as Max came up the stairs,
Daisy lost her balance on the chair and,
with a loud yell, fell down onto Max. The
bucket toppled over, soaking them both
from head to toe in icy cold water.

At that moment James appeared.

"Say cheese!" James laughed, and before they could escape, he had snapped Daisy and Max with his camera!

Carnival Crasher

Molly was going to be a majorette in the town carnival. But there was bad news. "I'm sorry," said Mrs. Ellis, the majorette coach. "All our batons have disappeared, so we can't rehearse today."

That evening, Molly's dad came home early from his band rehearsal. "Someone has stolen some of our instruments!" he said, sounding very angry. "If we don't get them back, there won't be any music for the parade. The carnival will have to be cancelled."

The next day, Molly went to see Mrs. Ellis. "Have you found our batons yet?" she asked.

"I'm afraid not, Molly," Mrs. Ellis replied.

As Molly turned to leave, she saw a trophy sitting on a shelf. It was last year's Carnival Queen trophy, and it belonged to Mrs. Ellis's daughter, Susie. Molly picked it up.

"Don't touch that!" said Susie, walking into the room.

"Susie is very proud of her trophy," said Mrs. Ellis. "But she's got to give it away soon."

"Why?" asked Molly.

"The new Carnival Queen will want it," replied Mrs. Ellis.

"If the carnival happens, that is," muttered Susie under her breath.

Molly overheard what Susie said. "I wonder...?" she thought to herself. "Perhaps this explains why everything's been disappearing!"

"Er... may I use your bathroom please, Mrs. Ellis?" asked Molly. She ran upstairs. Quickly she looked around to check that no one had seen her, then she crept into Susie's bedroom.

Molly spotted a pile of batons under the bed. Something shiny was sticking out of a closet. Molly opened the door, and a trombone fell out.

Molly went downstairs holding the trombone and a baton. "Are these yours, Susie?" she asked.

Susie burst into tears. "I wanted to be the Carnival Queen forever," she cried. "That's why I wanted to stop this year's carnival. I'll make it up to everyone, I promise!"

"You certainly will, Susie!" said her mom angrily.

Susie sniffed loudly. "I know," she said. "I could do face-painting for all the children in the parade."

"Well, that's a start," said her mom.

Susie's face-painting was a huge success. Just before the parade started, Susie presented her trophy to Tiffany, the new Carnival Queen. "Congratulations!" she said. "It's good being a Carnival Queen, but it's even more fun being a make-up artist!"

Egyptian Job

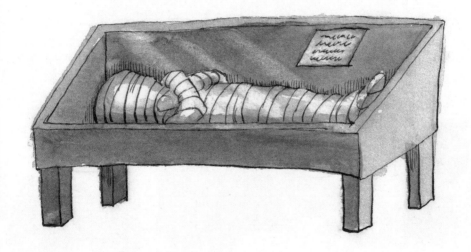

Eddie and Josh were counting all
the money they had made by doing
odd jobs.

"It's nowhere near enough to buy our
bikes yet," Eddie said gloomily.

His mom came into the room. "I've got another odd job for you both!" she said. "I need people to hand out leaflets tomorrow." Eddie's mom ran the store at the local museum.

The next morning, Eddie and Josh went to the museum with Eddie's mom.

She gave them a big pile of leaflets about the new Egyptian mummy exhibition.

"Give these to the people walking by" she said.

It was a freezing cold day. Eddie
and Josh were soon cold and tired.

"My fingers are like blocks of ice!"
moaned Josh.

233

"Let's go inside," said Eddie. "We can hide in the bathroom while we get warm again."

A cleaning cart had been left in the bathroom. On top of it were two huge rolls of toilet paper.

Eddie looked at Josh and smiled. He picked up one of the rolls and began to wrap it around and around Josh.

"This will keep you warm!" he joked.

When Eddie had finished, Josh could hardly move.

"You look very funny!" laughed Eddie, giving Josh a friendly push.

Josh lost his balance and fell against the bathroom door. The door opened and he staggered through it. "Help!" he yelled.

In front of him, a mummy display case was open. Two robbers were about to steal the priceless mummy.

"Aaargh!" screamed the robbers, seeing Josh. "That mummy has come to life!"

Josh, who was still trying to regain his balance, staggered towards them.

"Quick! Let's get out of here!" the robbers cried.

The manager hurried over to Josh and Eddie. "You've saved our prize exhibit!" he said. "You deserve a reward! I am writing you each a check for $200."

"Wow!" said Josh.

"Now we have enough money to buy our bikes!" said Eddie.

Lost in the Ocean

"I'm going to take some photos of sharks," said Mom one morning. "Do you two want to come with me?"

"Yes, please!" said Lili and Zac together. They smiled at each other.

Mom got her camera, and then they all got into the boat and set sail.

Zac was the first to see the sharks. "There they are!" he pointed.

"Look at that one. It's leaping!"
gasped Lili.

Zac and Lili loved watching the sharks.

Mom took lots of photos. "I can't wait
to go home and print them out," she
said happily.

But Mom had been so busy following
the sharks she'd sailed too far into the
ocean. "Never mind, I'll find the way
home soon," she told Lili and Zac.

Then it started to get foggy. The fog came down so thick it was hard to see in front of them.

"Oh no, I think we're lost," said Mom.

Some whistles and squeaks sounded out nearby. Dark shapes bobbed around in the water, at the side of the boat, whistling loudly.

"Dolphins," said Mom.

The dolphins swam around the boat, whistling and leaping out of the water.

"What are they doing?" asked Zac.

"I think they want to show us the way home," said Mom. "I've heard stories of dolphins helping people lost in the ocean."

Then they heard a familiar clicking sound.

It was Whistler, the dolphin they had once saved.

Whistler kept very close to the boat. Mom followed him and the other dolphins through the fog until at last the jetty came into view.

"I think Whistler and his friends guided us home to say thank you for helping them before," Zac said, as they climbed out of the boat.

"I think you're right," agreed Mom.

245

"You're great, Whistler!" called Zac.

"Thanks, Whistler!" shouted Lili. They all waved goodbye as the dolphins swam away from the beach, whistling and jumping out of the water.

Daisy the Detective

Daisy wanted to be a detective.
She had a little note book and a
magnifying glass.

Daisy looked at things through her
magnifying glass. Then, she wrote down
notes in her book.

247

"What are you doing, Daisy?" asked her little sister, Rose.

"I'm looking for clues," smiled Daisy. She pointed to the soft dirt underneath the rose bushes. "Can you see those footprints? They belong to a lion."

"You can see where he walked across the yard. He must have escaped from the zoo," said Daisy.

"How do you know all this?" asked Rose.

"I'm a detective," said Daisy. "I hunt for clues." Daisy pulled some fur from a thorn on one of the rose bushes.

"Look at this clue!" said Daisy. "This is lion fur. The lion passed by here. He left his footprints in the dirt, and he caught his fur on that thorn. Next, he went over to the tree. He could be up there watching us right now."

Up in the tree, Daisy's cat Ginger lay on a branch, asleep.

Daisy spotted some smoke coming from Mr. Brown's yard high above the fence.

"Look!" Daisy said to her sister. "You see! There's another clue. It's a dragon. They breathe fire and smoke."

"Really?" asked Daisy's sister. Her eyes opened wide with fright.

"Yes," said Daisy. "I'm a detective and I know how to hunt out clues."

Behind the fence, Mr. Brown lifted more leaves onto his bonfire.

Just then, Mom called out from the kitchen.

"Daisy! Rose! Could you come here?" The two sisters ran to the back door.

"We've been following clues, Mom!" said Rose. "Did you know that we've had a lion and a dragon in our yard?"

"Really?" said Mom. "Well, if you know all that, maybe you know where the cookies have gone? There are none left in the jar."

"Someone must have taken them," said Rose. "But don't worry. Daisy is a great detective." Rose turned to her sister. "Do you know who did it, Daisy?"

"I'm not sure," mumbled Daisy. She half turned away from her mom and her sister, and then she pulled out her pocket. Secretly, Daisy shook a pile of crumbs onto the path. Then she smiled.

"I'm sorry," said Daisy. "I don't have a clue."

The Trouble with Lionel

Imagine a town filled with dragons
. . . riding around on bicycles, speeding
around on skateboards, walking to
school. The town would be filled with
interesting dragons—and no dragon was
more interesting than Lionel!

Lionel was only a small dragon, but he had a big problem. Each time he sneezed or coughed or laughed, flames would leap out of his mouth and set fire to everything around him.

Once, at the town fair, Lionel laughed, and set off all the fireworks!

Even Lionel's last birthday party was a disaster. When he tried to blow out the

candles on his cake, the flames toasted
the cake, burst the balloons, set fire
to the party hats, and melted all the
ice cream.

Lionel's other dragon friends, Dipsy,
Droopy, and Donald, were all able
to control the amount of flames they
breathed out. They could light a match or
cook dinner. But Lionel could not.

"Try holding your breath," said Dipsy.

"Try keeping your mouth shut," was Droopy's helpful comment.

"I've got the perfect thing," said Donald, and he tied his scarf around Lionel's jaw.

For a while the scarf worked. Then Lionel got an attack of the hiccups. Everyone ran for cover as a huge wall of flame burst out of Lionel's mouth. In an instant it burned down the town hall.

From that day on, Lionel wore a special mouthguard made out of fireproof material.

Then, one day, the four friends were given a special job to do.

Far away, a wicked witch flew through the streets at night on her broomstick keeping everyone awake. And she turned the local cats and dogs into mice and toads.

The young dragons practiced their skills. Except Lionel. He wasn't allowed to practice.

Soon, the four young dragons set off, flying high above the fields and farms until they reached the town. They camped out in a huge cave . . . and waited until it was getting dark.

The dragons watched the witch swoop over the town, chanting her magic spells. They knew they had to put a stop to the witch's tricks.

Dipsy shot out a flame at her, but it wasn't long enough. Then Droopy aimed at her broomstick, but missed! Donald tried surrounding the witch with a circle of fire, but she flew right through the middle of it.

The dragons quickly untied Lionel's mouthguard.

"Go on, Lionel!" they cried. Lionel blew a huge flame up into the sky. It surrounded the witch's broomstick.

The four friends watched as the witch fell and landed in a tree. They all cheered.

When the dragons arrived back home, Lionel was the hero of the hour. And he was able to celebrate, without his mouthguard!

Well Really, Sam!

It was Tuesday morning at Rush Hill School, Mrs. Barton was busy taking attendance, and Sam was late.

"Mrs. Barton" said Marty, "I saw Sam playing with the janitor's dog earlier."

263

Suddenly, Sam burst through the door and rushed in.

"You're late, Sam," Mrs. Barton said.

"Please, Mrs. Barton," said Sam, excitedly, "a huge monster leaped out of nowhere. It poked out its gigantic tongue and licked my face. Then it ran off."

"Sit down, Sam. I'd better have a word with your mom," Mrs. Barton sighed.

On Wednesday, Sam was late again.

"Mrs. Barton," said Alice. "I saw Sam playing in the sandbox, as I was walking across the playground."

Then, Sam opened the classroom door.

"Please, Mrs. Barton" gasped Sam, "I was coming across the playground when, suddenly, the ground opened up and I fell into an enormous hole. Then there was a rumble and I was thrown out of the hole. It closed up behind me, I ran across the playground, and here I am."

"Sit down, Sam. I really must talk to your mother," Mrs. Barton muttered.

The next day, Sam was late.

"Mrs. Barton," said Becky. "I saw Sam going into the candy store on his way to school."

Just then, Sam rushed in.

"Please, Mrs. Barton," panted Sam, "I was walking down the street, when I felt myself being sucked towards an alien spaceship. The aliens made me eat all this alien food, then I ran to school."

"Sit down, Sam," snapped Mrs. Barton, "Please ask your mother to come and see me tomorrow morning."

The next morning, when Mrs. Barton began to take attendance, several hands shot into the air. "Mrs. Barton, Sam's not here." Mrs. Barton sighed loudly.

At that moment, the door flung open.

"Please Mrs. Barton," Sam gasped, "there was a flood in our kitchen, and it was all my hamster's fault."

"Well really, Sam!" said Mrs. Barton. "That's quite enough of your stories. And I thought I told you to ask your mother to come and see me."

"Good morning, Mrs. Barton," said Sam's mom, poking her head around the door. "I'm sorry Sam was late this morning, but our hamster escaped last night. It got under the floorboards upstairs and chewed through the plastic water pipe. When we got up this morning, the whole kitchen was flooded."

"But it's cleared up now," smiled Sam, "and I won't be late again. I think I've had enough of adventures."

"Really, Sam?" grinned Mrs. Barton. "So have I!"

Lost in the Snow

Billy and Bobby were two sheepdogs. They lived on a farm in the hills. Their job was to help the farmer, Joe Kinley, bring the sheep safely in from the fields.

Early one snowy day, the two dogs woke up in their basket.

Joe came in to the kitchen. "Brrr … it's icy this morning, boys," he said.

After breakfast, the dogs ran around trying to keep warm, while Joe cleaned the house.

"Oh, no! I've forgotten to buy enough wood for the fire!" Joe exclaimed, suddenly. "I'd better get it right away."

The wood was sold in a store in a valley over the other side of the hill. It would take Joe all afternoon to walk there and back. "You'll have to bring the sheep in on your own today," he told Billy and Bobby. "I'll see you here tonight."

Joe gave the dogs a pat, put on his jacket and stepped out into the yard.

Soon the two dogs reached the big field where the sheep were huddled together.

Suddenly, Bobby heard a yelp behind him. Billy had stumbled into an icy hole.

"Are you hurt badly?" Bobby asked.

"I don't think I can walk right," said
Billy, struggling through the snow.

"I'll take the sheep to the farm, and come
back to help you as soon as I can," said
Bobby.

As soon as Bobby had rounded up the
sheep, he returned to find Billy.

But Billy wasn't in the field. He seemed to have disappeared into thin air. Bobby decided to go get Joe.

"Bobby!" said Joe, back at the house. "We were getting worried about you."

Bobby saw Billy in his basket beside the fire in the living room. He had a bandage around his leg.

"Thank goodness you're safe," said Bobby. "How did you get back?"

Billy explained that Joe had found him in the field on his way home after getting the wood. He had carried Billy and the wood home.

As they fell asleep, Bobby and Billy forgot about their day in the snow. Both dogs were dreaming of a cozy day at home infront of the fire.

Madison's Fairy Godmother

Madison looked in the store window.

"Oh," she sighed, "it's beautiful!"

"And look at the ballet shoes," said her sister Katie.

Madison had just started ballet lessons, and the dress and the shoes would be perfect! When Madison got home she asked Mom about the ballet dress and shoes. "You should see them, Mom," said Madison, "they're beautiful!"

"I can't afford to buy them right now," said Mom. "Maybe in a few months."

"A few months isn't long," said Dad, when he saw Madison's disappointed face. "Unless," he added jokingly, "you find yourself a fairy godmother."

"Like Cinderella," thought Madison. "But how do I find one? I'll send a note up the chimney."

Katie agreed to help Madison write it.
Then Katie sent the note up the chimney.

Madison was sure it would work. "I'll
know my fairy godmother when she
comes," she said to Katie. "She'll be
beautiful, with a white dress and wings."

The next week, Aunt Dolly came to stay.
Aunt Dolly was Madison's favorite aunt.

"But there's no way she's my fairy godmother," said Madison to Katie. "Not with the name Dolly!" Madison started to look at people for signs. Wings hidden beneath a coat? A magic wand in a pocket?

Grandpa came over for lunch on the weekend. Of course, it couldn't be him! Fairy godmothers aren't men!

And it wasn't Mrs. Jenkins, who lived next door.

The next day, Madison saw her Mom ironing a long white dress in the kitchen!

While Madison was playing in the backyard, she saw Grandpa in the garage, and he was sticking sparkly things onto what looked like a pair of white wings! Later, she saw Mrs. Jenkins riding her bicycle back from the store. She had a wand sticking out of the basket on her bicycle!

It was very mysterious.

The days passed, and still Madison's fairy godmother hadn't appeared.

"Do you know what?" Madison said to Katie, "the ballet dress and shoes are gone from the store window. Somebody must have bought them."

The next evening at bedtime, Madison asked Aunt Dolly to read her a story.

When Aunt Dolly came into Madison's bedroom, she was wearing a long white dress and a pair of sparkly white wings, and she was carrying a wand!

"These are for you," smiled Aunt Dolly.

And she gave Madison the ballet dress and pink shoes!

"You are my fairy godmother!" laughed Madison, kissing her aunt. The dress and shoes fitted perfectly.

When she went downstairs Mom told Madison that Aunt Dolly was going to a costume party, which explained why Mom had been ironing the dress and Grandpa had been making the wings.

"So, real people can be fairy godmothers too!" laughed Madison.